JULIA'S
Vaulting Dream

Alison Gieschen

ISBN: 1492187895
ISBN 13: 978-1492187899

Library of Congress Control Number: 2013915568
CreateSpace Independent Publishing Platform
North Charleston, South Carolina

This book is dedicated in loving memory of Doris Dyer, a wife, mother and grandmother who touched our lives and our hearts and whose contributions to the sport of vaulting will always be remembered.

CHAPTER ONE

Julia's mom tiptoed into Julia's room and sat on the edge of her bed. She gently touched Julia's shoulder.

"Time to wake up, sleepyhead. It's time for school."

Julia's eyes fluttered open, and suddenly, she sat upright in bed.

"Momma, I had the same dream again," Julia said with excitement.

"What dream is that, honey?"

"Well, I know this sounds crazy, but in my dream, I'm standing on the back of a cantering horse. My arms are up like this," she explained, holding her arms out to each side. "The sun is shining on my face, and the wind is blowing through my hair. I feel so happy and free, almost like I'm flying!" she described with a big smile on her freckled face. Her brown eyes looked up toward her mother and were lit up as she described her dream.

Her mom rustled the soft brown curls of her long hair and then stood up and walked over to her bedroom wall, which was decorated with several horse posters. "You've loved horses ever since you were a baby, Julia. I took you to a horse farm where we used to live in California to see them sometimes. I would let you pat their warm, soft noses, and you even got to sit on them a few times. Even as a baby you were never afraid of those big animals, and the dream you've been having isn't so far-fetched. When you were about two years old, we went

1

to the farm, and there was an equestrian vaulting competition being held there."

"What's equestrian vaulting?" Julia asked.

"It's a sport where people do gymnastics on the back of a moving horse. You saw people standing, just like you showed me," she said while stretching her arms out to the sides, level with her eyes. "But I can't believe you have those memories, because you were so little when you saw that."

"Wow," Julia exclaimed. "In my dreams, it seemed so real, like I was really there."

"It must have made quite an impression on your little mind," her mom laughed.

"Why haven't you taken me to see it again?" Julia asked.

"We moved when you were three, and as far as I know, there are no vaulting clubs around here. It never crossed my mind that you would take an interest in vaulting."

"Momma!" Julia burst out with excitement. "You promised I could take riding lessons this summer. Can you please try to find out if there are any places I could try vaulting around here? I just have to stand on a horse now that I know it's something people really do! You don't understand how happy it would make me, Momma," Julia pleaded.

"We'll see, honey. I'll try and find the time to look into it, but right now you need to get up and get ready for school."

"Promise you'll try to find it?"

"Promise," her mom replied.

Julia jumped out of bed and hurried to start her day. She couldn't believe that her dream was something she had seen once in real life. She was not going to let this drop. As she brushed her teeth, she started hatching a plan on how to make her dream a reality.

CHAPTER TWO

Julia's fourth-grade teacher had assigned a paper to the class. The students had to research a topic, include pictures, and write down where they got their information. Several girls in the class, the "horse-crazy group" her teacher called them, wanted to write their papers about horses. Her teacher was tired of reading about horses, so she told them to pick another topic. She wanted them to research something new. The group of four girls wrinkled their noses and grumbled among themselves, but Ms. Berrios held her ground and rattled off several topics that might be interesting for the girls to research. Julia had picked women astronauts as a backup, but she was not thrilled with the topic.

The morning of her dream, Julia got to school and went straight to Ms. Berrios. She walked up to her nervously as Ms. Berrios sat at her desk, grading papers.

"Ms. Berrios," she quietly and shyly called to get her teacher's attention.

"Yes, Julia, what can I do for you?"

"It's about the research paper."

"I hope you aren't going to ask me if you can write about horses again, because I already told you that you need to research something you don't know anything about, something new."

"Actually, I do have a topic I would like to write about. It does have to do with horses, but it's a sport I just learned about called equestrian vaulting."

Julia explained her dream to Ms. Berrios and how her mom told her that morning that her dream came from a memory she had of seeing the sport when she was just an infant. She told her teacher how much she wanted to learn about this sport and asked if she could "please, please" write about it for her report.

"Hmmm," her teacher mumbled, her hand on her chin and a thoughtful look on her face. She stared at Julia for a minute and drummed her fingers on the desk. Julia waited, her hands held together in front of her, whispering, "Please, please, please," silently. Julia held her breath.

Finally Ms. Berrios gave her answer. "I guess it would be OK since the report is about a sport on horses, and one that I have never even heard of before."

Julia let out a huge breath, and an enormous grin stretched across her face. "Thank you, Ms. Berrios! This will be the best report ever, I promise," she yelled over her shoulder as she ran off to tell her horse-crazy friends the exciting news.

Her friends were jealous, of course, when she told them the story, but they were also interested in learning about vaulting too. They knew about jumping, dressage, and English and Western riding, but like Julia, they had never even heard of equestrian vaulting.

That morning, Julia got all of her math and science done as quickly as possible so that she would have extra time on the computer to start researching her topic. Her heart was thudding in her chest, and she had a case of the butterflies when she finally got to sit down at the computer and type the words "equestrian vaulting" into Google.

CHAPTER THREE

Tons of pictures sprang up in front of Julia's eyes. She could not believe her dream was real. People of all ages, sizes, and shapes were performing on the backs of moving horses. The horses were all different colors, sizes, and breeds. Some pictures even showed two or three people on the back of one horse, all at the same time. Julia really wanted to see a video of vaulting, but all the videos were on YouTube, and the students were not allowed to go on that site. Soon several of her friends were gathered around her computer, looking over her shoulder, and even Ms. Berrios came over to see what all the buzz was about.

"OK, kids, you'll need to wait and see Julia's report, so go back to your own work, please," she said, shooing the students back to their seats.

"Can I make a suggestion?" Ms. Berrios asked Julia.

"Sure," Julia replied.

"Why don't we see if we can find a site that will give you information about the sport, instead of just pictures?"

Ms. Berrios and Julia looked together, and sure enough, they found the organization that ran the sport of vaulting in the United States. It was called the American Vaulting Association, or the AVA.

"Jackpot!" yelled Julia.

Ms. Berrios shushed her, smiled, patted Julia's shoulder, and left her to her research. The website had all kinds of information about the sport (even about its history and how it got started). It even had facts about how safe it was, information about vaulting horses, pictures, videos, and every other detail you might want to know about vaulting. Julia was more than excited when she saw the link that read, "Find a club." She knew this was not the time to look up that type of information, with Ms. Berrios looking over her shoulder, and would save that search until she got home to her own computer.

That day, Julia spent every spare minute looking up her topic. By the time she left school, she had two pages written. She had the rest of the week to finish writing and put her report together to present it to the class. She would use her computer at home to do more research and watch as many videos as she could to get a feel of what vaulting was really like.

After running off the bus and sprinting to her house, Julia burst through the front door.

"Momma, Momma, are you home?" Julia yelled into the front hallway.

"Of course, I am," her mother replied, coming out of the kitchen, wiping her hands on her apron. Julia didn't even comment on the smell of freshly baked cookies coming from the kitchen. Normally she would have run right past her mom and into the kitchen to grab a warm and buttery cookie off the cooling rack.

"What has you all in a tizzy?" asked her mother.

"Ms. Berrios let me change the topic for my research paper to equestrian vaulting! I already started researching it at school today. I can't wait to show you what I found on the computer," she gushed with excitement.

"Just hold your horses," her mom said, laughing at her own joke. "Come have a warm cookie and a drink, get your homework done, and then we can look at the computer. I need to clean up from my baking anyway."

"Aw, Mom," Julia complained.

"Sorry, dear, homework comes first, and then you can go on the computer."

"But this *is* homework," Julia argued.

Her mother gave her a stern look, and Julia knew the discussion was over. Marching into the kitchen, she slung her book bag on the back of the chair and sat down with a thump.

An hour later, Julia's snack and homework were finished, and so she resumed begging for her mom to look at the computer with her. Her mom agreed, and the two of them went into the den and booted up the computer.

Julia had memorized the website address, www.american-vaulting.org. Her mom was impressed. Julia pulled up the site and right away pointed to the link about how to find a vaulting club in the area. Each area of the country was divided into regions, and Julia was able to find their region.

"You know, Julia, just because there might be a club around us does not mean you can definitely do vaulting. I don't have any idea how much this sport costs or if you need to have taken gymnastics or what is involved in joining a club. At least with riding lessons, I know what's involved. I know how much it costs and that you can do it just for the summer."

"But, Momma, you promised you would look into it for me," Julia pleaded, not wanting to believe her mother would give up this easily.

"I didn't say I wouldn't, Julia. I just don't want to get your hopes up too much yet." She looked at Julia sternly, and Julia nodded, swallowing hard. "All right then," her mom said, "let's see if there even are any clubs in our area."

CHAPTER FOUR

Julia was ecstatic when she and her mom found a club less than an hour away from their house. Julia's mom said it would be a long drive but doable and promised to call to find out more information. There was about a month of school left before summer vacation, and Julia's mom told her she would, at the very least, have to wait until school was out before trying vaulting. Julia was OK with that as long as there was vaulting somewhere in her future. Julia's mom took down the phone number of the nearest club from the AVA website, but when she called, there was a message saying that the team was away at a competition and would not be back for two weeks. Julia hated waiting, but at least she had her report to keep her busy.

As Julia waited for the team to return, she pictured what vaulting would look like when she finally got to see it in person. She worked very hard on her report for school. She had never been so excited about giving a presentation. She wrote her paper, gave the sources where she got the information, and made a poster. Also, she asked Ms. Berrios if she could use the SMART Board to show pictures and a video. Her teacher agreed, and that was icing on the cake for Julia's report. She was sure she was going to get an A+. The best part about it was that she was learning so much about the sport that she would be able to answer any questions her parents might have about vaulting. Every night before she went to bed, she pictured herself standing on a cantering horse, arms spread out like an eagle's wings and the wind blowing through her hair.

The day finally arrived for Julia to give her report to the class. Ms. Berrios had drawn names, and Julia was the third to go. She was so excited, she would have been more than happy to go first. The first two reports given by her classmates were about Jane Goodall, the lady who studied gorillas, and white tigers and how they are endangered. Julia fidgeted until it was finally her turn to go. As promised, Ms. Berrios set up the SMART Board so that, when ready, Julia could go online and show pictures and the video about vaulting.

Julia walked up to the front of the room with her paper in hand, ready to read, and a small poster board with facts and pictures. When she opened her mouth to start speaking, she was so nervous that her mouth went dry, and suddenly, she couldn't speak. She tried very hard to swallow, but there was not one drop of saliva in her mouth. Her face turned bright red with embarrassment, and a few kids started to chuckle in the back of the class.

"Are you OK, Julia?" Ms. Berrios asked with concern.

Julia nodded and took a deep breath and told herself to relax. She hadn't realized just how important this report was to her until now. After a few moments of deep breathing, she was ready to begin.

Julia began with some facts about the history of vaulting. She explained that, through vaulting, soldiers were trained to fight from many different positions on horseback before going to battle. She could tell the boys in the class found that interesting, because they looked up from their doodling and note passing to pay attention to her.

"Yeah," she added in their direction, not from her paper, "can you guys imagine how cool it would be if you were a soldier fighting from your horse and you could jump on and off your horse while it was cantering, or fight standing up?"

A few of the boys nodded. Then she explained more about vaulting history and how it became a sport because it was so much fun. It was included in the very first Greek and Roman Olympic Games. Then Ms. Berrios interrupted her with a question.

"Why isn't vaulting in the Olympics now, Julia?"

Julia was ready for that question and quickly answered, "The Olympic Games started making rules about how many countries there needed to be for a sport to be in the Olympics. Vaulting didn't have enough countries, so it was dropped. The good news is that there are enough countries for it to be considered, so there's a petition for it to be put back in the games. I hope they do, because I want to be an Olympic vaulter someday," Julia said with a big smile.

Several kids laughed at her, and she turned red in the face again. She looked at Ms. Berrios, who said, "Sorry for interrupting you, Julia. Please go on with your report."

Next she told the class that hundreds of riding stables use vaulting to help people with all different kinds of handicaps. She even read that vaulting was being used to help soldiers after they came back from war. She was very careful to put the facts in her own words when she gave her report, just like Ms. Berrios had taught the class to do.

Then she talked about vaulting being a competitive sport. She explained that vaulting is done while the horse is walking, trotting, and cantering. There is a piece of equipment called a surcingle that goes around the horse's middle and has handles that the vaulters use to mount the horse while it is moving and to hold on to as they do moves on the horse. The horses are very well trained and are going around in a circle. There is a person in the center of the circle, called a lounger, holding onto a long rope called a lounge line. The lounger stands in the middle of the circle while holding the lounge line and a very long whip, which is used to keep the horse steady and controlled at all times. There is also a piece of equipment called a barrel for training. It has handles on it, just like a surcingle, and vaulters practice their routines on it and do lots of training to help them be better vaulters on the horse. They can even enter barrel classes at the competitions.

Then she explained, pointing to her poster, that there were compulsory exercises and freestyles in vaulting. All vaulters trained in compulsories, and everyone who competes has to do these exercises. This teaches the vaulters balance, rhythm, and how to move with the horse's gait. She gave a list of the basic moves and then explained how the compulsory exercises are modified or made easier for vaulters in the lower levels. All vaulters have to do these moves and get a score from one to ten on each move.

The vaulting levels Julia described started with horse walking for beginners. Even someone at the walk stage could go to a competition. The next level was trot, and then there were four levels of canter: copper, bronze, silver, and gold. Gold was the highest level. Canter level vaulters sometimes have opportunities to attend vaulting competitions called CVIs which are international competitions. If a vaulter becomes one of the top vaulters in the country, he or she could be picked to go the Vaulting World Championships.

Next Julia talked about freestyles. In freestyles, vaulters get to pick which exercises they want to do, and they put together a one-minute routine set to music and performed like a dance on horseback. Julia described it as a cross between dance and gymnastics, because while they are dancing, vaulters do rolls, cartwheels, splits, handstands, and many other gymnastic-type moves. Julia pointed to her poster and showed pictures of each compulsory exercise and a few of vaulters doing their freestyles.

"One more vaulting event is called team freestyle. I would like to show you some pictures from the Internet and a video of a team freestyle," Julia said to her classmates. She could see all the eyes of her classmates as they hung on her every word, eager to see what she would talk about next.

Julia tapped on the SMART Board, and a picture of three people on a giant horse filled the screen. Her classmates broke out in chatter when they saw the picture.

"Quiet down, everyone, Julia will explain everything," Ms. Berrios told the class.

"This is team vaulting. Six people are on a team and do a four-minute freestyle routine to music, and up to three people can be on the horse at the same time. There are bases, the strong ones who support the other vaulters, and flyers. Flyers are the smaller people who are held up by the bases."

Next Julia tapped the board, and a video came to life of a winning team freestyle being performed at a national competition. The kids were silent as they watched, mouths slightly open; some kids were even holding their breath as the vaulters mounted, pulled up their teammates, and performed difficult moves on the cantering horse, with graceful arm movements that matched the tempo and beats of the music.

When the video ended, Julia turned to the class and said, "And that is equestrian vaulting."

Hands shot up in the air as soon as Julia finished her report. Ms. Berrios wanted students to ask questions after each report, but Julia had never seen so many hands up at once. She broke out in a big smile, knowing that her report had been excellent, and she began answering the many questions.

CHAPTER FIVE

Julia rushed home from school, knowing her mom was going to make the call to the Sunrise Vaulters sometime after dinner. After clearing the table and helping with the dishes, Julia sat quietly in the corner of the kitchen so she could listen to the conversation. Her mom still had the phone number from the AVA website, and she called it and asked to talk to the coach of Sunrise Vaulters. Julia's mom introduced herself and asked the many questions she had about vaulting. Julia listened and shook her head back and forth when her mom asked, "But isn't it dangerous?"

She had told her mom a hundred times that vaulting was safer than riding horses—or soccer, gymnastics, bike riding, or even cheerleading. Julia guessed that she had to hear that fact from another adult to believe it. Her mom also asked if it was OK that Julia had never taken gymnastics, and her mom listened as Miss Carol explained that gymnasts made great vaulters, but anyone could learn to vault and be good at it. The last question Julia's mom asked was one that Julia was most worried about. Julia knew that her parents didn't have a lot of money, and it was one of the reasons Julia had not taken riding lessons before now. Riding lessons were very expensive, and Julia knew that money might be the one reason she could never vault. Her parents had told her that they would never have enough money to buy and keep her own horse. The best they could do was save-up for riding lessons over the summer.

Julia's mom asked about when the club practiced, what kind of clothing they wore, and what they did when it rained, but when she asked the question, "How much does vaulting cost?" Julia was so nervous she was sweating bullets. She sat in the corner of the kitchen, her arms wrapped tightly around her legs, and rocked back and forth. She couldn't hear Miss Carol's answer, but there was a lot of explaining going on. Her mom was listening carefully and answering, "I see, uh-huh. Yes. OK. Her father and I will discuss it and get back to you."

Julia's mom hung up the phone and walked into the kitchen. Julia was still curled tightly in her little ball. She looked up at her mom, and her eyes started to tear up. She had a horrible feeling her dreams of vaulting were about to come to an end. After all, how could something as wonderful as vaulting be affordable for a little girl like her?

"Why are you sad, Julia?" her mom asked with surprise.

"I'm scared you're going to tell me I can't try vaulting because it's going to cost too much," Julia said, almost in tears.

"Come here, baby," Julia's mom said, pulling her up from the corner where she sat and giving her a big hug. "I know this really means a lot to you, doesn't it?"

Julia could only nod because she was afraid she would start crying if she spoke. She looked up at her mom's face and searched for some sign that there was going to be good news.

Her mom began explaining, "The good news is that this vaulting program owns the horses, and the costs for the horse are shared by everyone on the team. That means that vaulting is less expensive than riding."

"Really?" Julia said, her hopes beginning to rise.

"Yes, really. However, if you plan on going to competitions, there are a lot more costs."

"Like what, and how much?" Julia wanted to know everything.

"Well, you have to buy special shoes for vaulting, and a uniform, and you have to pay to join the AVA, which is where we got all our information from. Then there are fees to compete, and vaulters share the costs for the horses to travel and stay and be stabled."

"That sounds really expensive," Julia said, looking down at the floor.

"Well, let's talk to your dad when he gets home. Miss Carol said that they go to a few competitions that are close to home that don't cost too much."

At least there is some hope I might get to be a vaulter and compete.

CHAPTER SIX

Summer had officially started, and on Julia's first week home from school, she had a plan. She printed out fliers for pet sitting and walked around town putting them in every shop window and street pole she could find. Her parents had agreed to let her try vaulting, but she had to raise her own money if she wanted to go to any competitions. Julia had spent hours watching videos of girls her age at vaulting competitions, and it was her dream not only to vault but to compete. Miss Carol had invited Julia to join practice the weekend after school let out. Julia had no idea what to expect on her first day there, but she decided to raise money early by starting a pet-sitting service just in case everything worked out.

By the end of the week, Julia had several people lined up for her pet-sitting services. As Julia drove with her mom to her first vaulting practice, Julia was more excited than a kid on Christmas morning. On the drive to the farm, Julia's mom gave her some advice.

"I know you're thrilled to be trying vaulting, Julia, but don't jump the gun on your goals to be a competitive vaulter just yet. Remember, we're just going to try it out."

"I know, Mom. But I've been working really hard, and I'm going to keep working all summer to make money in case I can go to a competition. There is nothing wrong with being ready, is there, Momma?"

"I'm just telling you not to get your hopes up too much just yet. You don't even know how hard this sport is or if you'll like it. What if you get on the horse, and vaulting scares you? Those horses look very big to me. You've never even taken a riding lesson, and you're jumping right into doing gymnastics on a horse!"

Julia closed her eyes and remembered the feeling from her dream. The horse cantered steadily with every step of his powerful gait. She stood, and her knees and feet melted into the rhythm of the canter. She felt one with the horse, a freedom and power greater than any feeling she had ever known. Somehow, she knew in her heart that she was meant to be a vaulter.

"Julia," her mom called out to her, waking her from her daydream. "We're here."

Julia's eyes flew open, and she saw an entrance to a farm with a white, yellow, and red sign that read, "Home of Sunrise Vaulters." It had a logo of a girl doing a handstand on a horse, with the words curving around the horse and vaulter.

Julia's eyes were as wide as dinner plates as she looked around, trying to take everything in at once. There were girls leading two horses from the barn toward a riding arena. The horses had vaulting surcingles and thick back pads, and the girls leading them were carrying the long lounge lines and whips in their hands.

In the riding arena—which looked like a beach with soft, white, deep sand—were vaulting barrels and some other equipment, like mini trampolines, Hula-Hoops, jump ropes, and yoga balls. Girls of different sizes and ages were milling around, and then a tall lady with curly brown hair and a straw hat gathered them all together in the arena and had them sit in a big circle. As Julia's mom parked the car, Julia jumped out and saw the vaulters straddle their legs and begin stretching exercises together. Miss Carol was the woman with the straw hat, and she walked over and introduced herself and then brought Julia and her mom over to join the group. The horses had been tied to the fence with halters and lead ropes and were waiting patiently for the practice to begin.

Julia and her mom approached the circle of stretching vaulters, and Miss Carol reached out for Julia's hand and pulled her into the middle of the circle.

"You must be Julia," she said with a welcoming smile.

Julia nodded, not wanting to speak in front of the group.

"Your mom says you're very excited to try vaulting, and we're so glad you came out to give it a try."

Miss Carol introduced Julia to the group and made each vaulter say their name and how long they had been vaulting. Julia was surprised that some of the other girls were also new to vaulting. One girl had only vaulted once before. She looked up at Julia and waved in a friendly way, and Julia waved back, knowing that she would feel safe hanging out with her on her first day. There were also trot, copper, silver, and even a gold-level vaulter on the team. Miss Carol told Julia to join in the circle and do the stretching exercises to be sure her muscles would be ready to vault. She made her way over and sat next to the other new girl. While she was following the lead of the other vaulters, Miss Carol and her mom went toward the horses.

Stretching was done, and the oldest vaulter, Katie, who was also the gold-level vaulter, took Julia under her wing and told her how the practice would work. There was a dry-erase board with stations written on it that the vaulting groups would rotate through. Julia would be in group one with the other newer vaulters. They would go to the barrel first, where someone would help them learn some drills and warm-up exercises, and then they would practice what they had learned on a moving horse. Julia could barely contain her excitement to get on her first vaulting horse.

CHAPTER SEVEN

So tired and happy after her first vaulting lesson, Julia fell asleep on the car ride home. It was Saturday afternoon, and her mother had put dinner in the Crock-Pot, and it would be ready to eat when they got home.

Julia's dad was setting out the dinner plates when Julia ran through the door yelling, "Dad, Dad, I vaulted today! And guess what? They said I was really good at it."

"Well, let's sit down to dinner, and you can tell me all about it," her dad said, wrapping his big arms around her and giving her a kiss on the forehead.

Julia and her mom helped set out dinner, and they sat down and said a blessing. Julia added, "And thank you for my wonderful first day of vaulting," at the end.

She then told her dad about how nice all the vaulters were to her and that they were all like one, big, happy family. She already knew she wanted to be just like Katie, the oldest and most experienced vaulter.

"And, Daddy, they let me stand today!"

"No way, not on your first day."

"Uh-huh. I told Katie about my dream and how I wanted to stand more than anything else in the world. Katie sat on the neck of the horse, facing backward, and I got on and held onto her shoulders, and she held on around my waist so that I wouldn't fall. Then I let go and put my arms out like this," she said while holding her arms out to the side. "It was only at the walk and then the trot, but, Daddy, it was just like my dream!"

Julia's mom and dad looked at each other and smiled.

"Weren't you afraid of the big horses?" her dad asked.

"Oh my gosh, Daddy, they were so gentle. I loved the horses so much. They were the best part of today. When I would stand next to them, they would bring their head right down to me, and I could look them right in the eyes. I patted their giant faces and felt their warm breath blowing on my face. They were so kind and gentle and well trained that they did everything they were told by the loungers. I could not believe how much I fell in love with them in just one day."

A month went by, and Julia attended vaulting practice twice a week. She practiced all her drills and her compulsories, and Katie even helped her make up her very own freestyle. One afternoon at practice, the team had a meeting. Sunrise Vaulters had been asked to do a demonstration at a county fair. Julia sat quietly, listening to the team plan what they wanted to do for the upcoming demonstration. Miss Carol looked at Julia and the other new vaulter and asked, "Would you girls like to demonstrate the compulsory exercises at the trot?"

Julia couldn't believe what she had just heard. She had only been vaulting a month, and she was being included in a big demonstration in front of hundreds of people.

"Really?" Julia asked. "I could do that?"

"Of course," Miss Carol answered. "The crowds would love to see how even vaulters new to the sport can learn harmony and balance in all different positions so quickly. They need to see vaulters of all ages and levels, and I'm so proud of how you two girls are coming along so quickly."

Julia was more than thrilled to be included in the vaulting demonstration. As soon as she got home that night, she called all her friends and told them the big news that she would be demonstrating vaulting at the county fair.

CHAPTER EIGHT

The summer months flew by, and Julia practiced as much as possible. Her team had given her extra stretching and strength exercises to do at home to help with her vaulting. Julia put a chart up in her room and checked off the ones she did every day. She was now able to do a full split, and her handstands were getting better every day. She was proud of how strong and flexible she was becoming, as those were just the skills she needed to become a really good vaulter. She smiled to herself when she thought about gym class and how doing forty curl ups, three pull ups and run a mile in nine minutes seemed like such a challenge in order to get the Presidential Fitness Award. She could now do three sets of fifty curl ups, five pull ups and run a mile in just over eight minutes. Vaulting had inspired her to get into great shape and she was enjoying seeing her fitness level improve.

Julia had also been working very hard at her pet-sitting job. She had made over three hundred dollars during the summer. She wanted to go to a competition in the fall, but there was one thing she wanted even more. For around $350, she could buy her very own vaulting barrel for her backyard so that she could practice vaulting every single day. Her parents told her that she had a decision to make. She could go to her first competition in September, or she could use her money to buy a barrel and be able to really practice her new skills. Julia could not make a decision.

The middle of August was Julia's birthday. For her birthday, she had asked Miss Carol if she could bring her friends to the farm and let them all sit on a vaulting horse. Her mom and dad said she was crazy for asking, but to her surprise, Miss Carol said, "Sure, you can have one horse to give your friends a short demo and then let them each try a compulsory move or two on the barrel and then the horse."

Julia thought she had died and gone to heaven, being able to show all her horse-crazy friends her vaulting horses and how she had followed her dreams. She was a real vaulter now.

Her birthday arrived, and five of her friends packed into her mom's minivan for the trip to the horse farm. The van pulled up, and the girls tumbled out of the doors. Julia gave them instructions on how to behave around the horses and told them they had to wait patiently until Miss Carol brought out the vaulting horse. Miss Carol came out to meet the group. She pulled Julia aside and told her, "Happy birthday, Julia. Before we begin, there's something I need to show you. Your mom and dad had me order a very special birthday gift for you."

Julia looked back at her mom and dad, who were standing by the van with the group of noisy girls.

"Go on, go with Miss Carol and see your birthday gift," her dad said with a big grin on his face.

Carol led Julia by the hand to the end of the arena. There was a brand-new vaulting barrel with a big bow tied to the handles. Julia stopped and stared at it with disbelief.

"It's mine? That's really my birthday present?" she asked, not believing what she was seeing.

"Yes, Julia, this is a gift from your parents."

Julia could not hold back her joy. She ran up and touched her barrel, ran back and hugged her coach, and then turned and sprinted back to where her parents were standing.

Shedding a few tears because she was so happy, she leapt into her dad's arms, "I love you so much, mom and dad. This is the best birthday present ever!"

CHAPTER NINE

September arrived, and Julia had saved enough money to pay for her first vaulting competition. She was going to be entered in the Preliminary Trot Division. She had also been practicing on the barrel so much that she decided to enter two barrel classes as well. There were going to be thirteen vaulters from her team at the Fall Vaulting Fest.

The day before the competition, all the vaulters had to go to the farm and help Miss Carol prepare. The horses had to be bathed and braided. Julia learned how to wash a horse and clean the equipment so that everyone, including the horses, would look their best. She loved working around the gentle giants and polishing their hooves and brushing out their tails. It was her time to bond with the horses.

Julia had a uniform that was handed down to her from another vaulter who had grown out of it. This saved her a lot of money because the new ones were quite expensive. She ordered brand-new vaulting shoes that she paid for with her birthday money. She also had her very own freestyle music ready, which she had been practicing her routine to for the last few weeks. Everything was ready for her to compete, and this was a dream come true for Julia.

The competition was at a horse park about two hours from Julia's house. All the team arrived there on Friday night and stayed in a hotel so that they could be ready bright and early on Saturday morning. On Friday evening, all the vaulters helped get the horses out of the horse trailer and into their stalls and put all the feed, hay, and vaulting equipment into a stall next to the horses. They proudly hung their Sunrise Vaulters banner on the door to their tack stall so that everyone would know which club they were among the many other clubs at the competition.

Saturday morning arrived, and Julia felt like a princess. She had all her teammates around her, putting her hair up in a tight bun and decorating it with tiny flowers and sparkles. All her teammates looked beautiful, like performers ready to amaze the judges with their wonderful vaulting routines. Her teammates really were like a big family. Every person on the team was helpful, especially for the newer members, and everyone watched and cheered on their teammates.

Finally it was Julia's turn to enter her first class. It was compulsories on the horse at the trot. She had Katie run into the ring with her to give her a boost onto the horse, as she had some trouble mounting easily yet. Julia followed Katie's footsteps as she jogged into the center of the vaulting arena, stood next to the horse and lounger, and bowed to the judge. It was what every vaulter did before and after vaulting. The judged nodded to Julia, and then the horse went out into its circle and began trotting. At the sound of a bell, Julia raised her hand for her music to begin playing, and she and Katie ran out to the trotting horse. Katie boosted Julia up on the horse effortlessly. They had worked together to get the timing just perfect to make it appear as if Julia floated as light as a feather onto the horse. Katie ran out of the circle, and Julia was left all alone, in front of the judge, for her first competitive round of vaulting. She raised her arms for basic seat and then popped up to her knees for flag. For a moment, her mind went totally blank, and her nerves took over. She returned to her seat instead of going up to stand. Sick to her stomach at her mistake, she quickly popped to her feet and stood tall with her arms stretched out to the sides for a perfect stand without a single bobble. She knew, however, that her mistake of sitting back down before going to stand was going to cost her points in her score. She completed her compulsories, dismounted, and lined up to bow to the judge. She could hear her teammates on the sidelines cheering, clapping, and supporting her in every possible way. She was so embarrassed when she ran out of the ring that she wanted to dig a hole and bury herself. How could she have forgotten the order of her compulsories? Everyone hugged her and told her what a great job she did and that it was very common for nerves to take over during a competition and people to make mistakes. They all told her not to worry about it and that she had an amazing round for her first time in front of a judge. Julia hugged her horse, thanked her lounger, and waved to her parents, who were so proud of their daughter and the fact that she had come so far in just a short time.

The rest of the weekend flew by, and Julia's last class was barrel freestyle. She had placed almost last in her compulsories on the horse and took tenth out of twelve vaulters in her freestyle on the horse. Barrel compulsories had gone well, and she was calm and ready for her last class. She was so focused and prepared that she did her routine the best she had ever done it. Julia waited nervously for the scores to be counted, and finally the results were posted. Julia's hard work and all her practice paid off. She took first place out of twelve vaulters in the barrel freestyle! She could not believe her eyes. Her teammates, coach, and parents were very happy for her and congratulated her on a job well done.

Julia collected all her ribbons for the weekend and helped prepare all the horses and equipment to be packed up and shipped home. It was a lot of work, but many hands helped get it done quickly. As they packed up their own car to leave, Julia's mom and dad took a moment to complement their daughter on how well she had done the whole weekend. They told her that they were never more proud of her than they were just now and how amazing she was to have worked so hard to follow her dreams and see them all come true.

CHAPTER TEN

Years passed, and Julia devoted just about every spare minute of her life to vaulting. She practiced on her barrel, she worked out and stretched, and she even took tumbling and dance classes to help with her vaulting skills. Julia went to lots of competitions and won all the divisions in trot, so she was moved up to canter. She did so well that they even put her in the team freestyle, which was another dream come true for Julia. She got to travel to different states and go to camps, clinics, and competitions. She made vaulting friends all over the country. Everyone, from her coach to her parents, was amazed at how quickly Julia learned the sport. It was as if she was always meant to be a vaulter. The best part for Julia was not winning ribbons, or even traveling to new places and making so many friends. Her favorite part was having her horse as her partner. She loved having him as a teammate and bonding and caring for such a special animal. Even though several other people on the team used the horse, her happy place was standing on a cantering horse. She was so good at standing that, when she stood, it was as if she was standing on the ground. She would spread her arms to the sky, as if she were flying, and let the sun shine on her face and the wind ripple through her hair. She would almost meld with her horse, and it was as if they were one. For Julia, there was no better feeling in the whole world and no place she would rather be.

Julia peeked around the corner and saw Ms. Berrios getting ready for homeroom. The children were coming into the room and talking with their friends and putting their books in their desks. Suddenly Ms. Berrios looked up and saw Julia's face peering around the doorway of the classroom.

"Ms. Berrios?" Julia greeted her former teacher.

"Yes?" she replied curiously.

"Hi, it's me, Julia. You were my teacher in the fourth grade. Do you remember me?" she asked with a big grin.

"Julia! Why, of course. How are you? I'm so happy you stopped by for a visit."

Julia entered the room. She had a blue ribbon with a shiny gold medal around her neck.

"Do you remember the report I gave at the end of the year on equestrian vaulting?"

"Of course, I do. That was one of the best fourth-grade reports I've ever seen, to this day. I still tell the kids about it at report time."

Kids drifted into the classroom and stared at the young lady talking to their teacher. Julia looked at them with a friendly smile as she chatted with Ms. Berrios.

"I see a ribbon around your neck with a vaulter on it," Ms. Berrios commented.

"This is why I came to visit you," Julia explained. "I owe this all to you. I learned so much from my vaulting report in this room that I just had to visit and tell you how much it changed my life. I wanted to say thank you," she said, tearing up and reaching to hug her former teacher.

The two of them shared a long embrace, and then Ms. Berrios asked a small favor from Julia.

"I want to hear all about your success, but would you mind sharing your vaulting story with my class? I talk about you all the time, and the kids would be thrilled to hear your story in person."

"Of course, Ms. Berrios. I would love to speak to your class."

After a few minutes, all the kids had settled, and Ms. Berrios introduced Julia to her class. She explained how many years ago, in that very room, a fourth grader named Julia did a research report on a topic that was new to her. It changed her life forever, and she told the kids that's why it's so important to learn about new things. You never know what doors it will open for you and what exciting things can be on the horizon if you just take the time to learn about them. It sure did for Julia, and with that, she sat down behind her desk and nodded for Julia to take the floor.

"Hi," Julia started. "I just want to say that you're very lucky to have the best fourth-grade teacher on the planet," she said with a big grin.

The kids clapped and cheered for their teacher, who waved her hand, as if to say, "Aw, shucks."

"I had a dream when I was your age. I dreamt I was standing on the back of a cantering horse, and I felt magical, like I was flying. When I woke up, I told my mom about the dream, and she explained that I had seen someone standing on a horse when I was very little. She said it was a sport called equestrian vaulting. It was time to do our research papers, so I asked Ms. Berrios if I could do my paper on vaulting, and she said yes. Because of that research, I found and joined a vaulting team. I started my own pet-sitting business so that I could raise money to go to competitions. I recently earned my gold medal, the highest honor there is in vaulting. With each of the levels in vaulting, you can take a test in front of the judge, and if you get high enough scores, you're awarded a medal at that level. I have all the medals in vaulting, trot, copper, bronze, silver, and now, finally, my gold medal. And my vaulting dreams are still coming true, as I was just picked to represent the United States in my first Vaulting World Championships in Germany."

The class oohed and aahed at this news.

"You see," she continued, "You have to work very hard to be one of the top vaulters in the country, because they only select three women and three men to represent the United States at the world-level competitions."

Julia looked over at Ms. Berrios, who was wiping the tears from her eyes for the pride she felt in being part of Julia's journey. A world-class athlete was standing there in her classroom.

"Vaulting has taken me all over our country, and to new countries, and I've had amazing experiences through this sport. I've learned to eat healthy and keep my body in the best possible shape. I've learned confidence, leadership, teamwork, and many other skills. Everyone in this room can find their own thing that makes them happy and allows them to experience life in a wonderful sort of way."

Then Julia paused, and then continued with a hint of emotion in her voice, "My wish for you is that you're as lucky as I have been to be able to follow my dreams. And if someday you want to feel like you're flying and the magic of dancing on horseback, I suggest you give vaulting a try."

The class exploded with clapping, and Ms. Berrios got up from her seat and gave Julia another hug.

"Gee, you've made me want to go out and try vaulting," Ms. Berrios said, only half joking.

"Well, Ms. Berrios, you're in luck. They even have vaulting classes for adults, called the Masters Class. Ms. Berrios, I'm giving you and all your students an open invitation to come and try vaulting at the Sunrise Vaulters Farm whenever you're ready."

The class cheered, Julia said her good-byes, and everyone wished her good luck at her biggest competition ever. She even gave them a website address where they could watch her vault on the Internet and see how she did. Then she headed out the door to her car, where her parents were waiting. They were headed to the airport to follow Julia's new dream of competing in the European Vaulting World Championships.

Born in upstate New York and raised on a hundred-acre horse farm, Alison Gieschen has been immersed in the horse world since childhood. She carried her passion for horses with her through her education at the University of North Carolina, where she earned a degree in English and met her husband, Daniel.

The couple then moved to New Jersey, built a farm, and started a family. Gieschen obtained teaching certifications from Rowan University, and has been teaching for the past fifteen years.

Through her roles as wife and mother, Gieschen was pulled even deeper into the horse world—introduced to polo when Daniel took it up, and to equestrian vaulting when their three-year-old daughter became fascinated with the sport. She has been coaching equestrian vaulting for over twenty years.

Now that their children are grown, Alison spends her time writing books to educate children about horses, combining her passion with her experience as a teacher and mother.

Manufactured by Amazon.ca
Bolton, ON

15982754R00031